# Ghosts

### of the

# Niagara River

# DEDICATION

I want to dedicate this book to my wife, Marilyn Carlson. She has put up with countless nights of my banging away on my old Underwood typewriter while writing this. She expected, and certainly deserved, some respite from that after previous books I have written. But, Ah, rest was not to come. She had to suffer through this one, also.

I also want to express my apprecia-appreciation to the many people who have been of invaluable help by sharing family records and personal experiences. Without that help, this book would be only a front and back cover. I owe a special thanks to The Local History Department of the Niagara Falls Public Library for their invaluable assistance.

# TABLE OF CONTENTS

# FOREWORD

All the folks who live or travel along The Niagara River are aware of things and places like both the city and the falls named Niagara Falls, Buffalo, and Grand Island. Most of them have at least heard of Goat Island and Youngstown.

But how many know about the image of Chad Swanson that appeared to his bride when she looked into the swirling waters at the base of the falls? How many know about the ghost that almost filled the canyon of The Whirlpool, or the soldiers in that old house between Lewiston and Old Fort Niagara?

Bruce Carlson's book GHOSTS OF THE NIAGARA RIVER is an immensely readable collection of ghost tales from this beautiful river.

There will undoubtedly be a few folks who are able to put this book down before finishing it. However, I don't think there will be many who can do it. Readers will be hooked on this book all the way through to the end of the last chapter.

> Professor Phil Hey
> Briar Cliff College
> Sioux City, Iowa

# PREFACE

The reader will find, in this book, a collection of tales about ghosts along the Niagara River.

The events described in this volume cover the period from the early 1800's to 1940. They are, however, not in chronological or any other order. Each story is a separate chapter, unrelated to any of the others.

Whenever possible, diligent effort was made to confirm these stories by getting information from other sources. That was, of course, not always possible. Ghost stories are often known to only a very small number of people.

The reader must appreciate the fact that, with only a couple of exceptions, none of these stories have ever been published before. Some of them could cause embarrassment to living people today. Because of that, some of the stories use fictitious names. In those cases, it should be understood that any similarity between those names and actual people, living or dead, is purely coincidental.

The author hopes that this book will serve to document some of the tales heretofore only handed down by word of mouth. They are part of the heritage of the beautiful Niagara River, and deserve to be preserved.

# CHAPTER I

## THE GHOST ON THE PHONE

**T**he bizarre situation that this tale tells is one that took place in a cow pasture outside of the city of Buffalo, New York in the 1870's. The tragedy of that otherwise beautiful June day is a part of, strangely enough, the history of the telephone in the United States.

The telephone was making its way from the order and security of the research laboratories cut into the rough-and-tumble environment of business offices and homes.

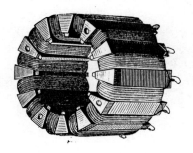

Some of the detractors of that new gadget would admit that it might work, but it would never work in the real world where people who were not engineers or technicians would be using it.

The records don't reveal to us who was sponsoring a dramatic piece of showmanship, but the usefulness of the telephone was going to be demonstrated in a very dramatic way. Two people, out of sight of each other, and on opposite sides of the Niagara River were going to actually talk to each other over that thing. There were going to be impartial observers present to be sure that the pair did not communicate with each other by some hidden means. The distance the two would be apart and the presence of the roar of the falls would be sufficient to demonstrate that the telephone could indeed, be a practical tool for business or personal use.

It was a clever idea, but it was never pulled off. In order to show that there was even promise for this new device in the home, it was decided to have a man

and a woman talk over it in the big demonstration. The couple who was going to conduct the show was a young couple that both had some theatrical experience so they could make the most of the drama of the event there on the banks of The Niagara River.

This couple were setting up to practice the telephone demonstration "in the field." They were doing so in a cow pasture out in the country southeast of Buffalo. A site had been chosen that would be accessible by road for all the gear, yet one where one end of the system could be around behind a hill from the other. The two could then go through the exercise of doing the practice run out of doors in a setting similar to that at the river where the public demonstration would take place.

It was an exciting thing to be doing. Not only were these two on the cutting edge of technology, but were being paid well for their efforts. This was important for the two of them planned to marry, and needed the money. They had, in fact, already picked out a set of china they had found in Buffalo that they were going to buy as soon as they were paid for the big show.

The story as I got it indicated that the young man's name was Walter Hickman. There is no information available as to the young lady's name. For the sake of convenience, I'll give her a name right now so we can talk about her. I'll call her Eunice.

The big day for the practice session came. Walter and Eunice were out at the site, getting all the equipment set up so they would have the telephones and the necessary testing equipment, power supply, etc. Everything had to go just right so that when they put the big show on over on the river, there wouldn't be any embarrassing slip-ups. They had even set them-selves up so they could wet the whole thing down and still use it in case it rained the day they were to put on the public demonstration.

Eunice was staying at the road with some engineers and Walter was walking back to his place around the hill. They were going to have some last minute conversations before they took the whole thing apart again prior to setting up over at the river.

Walter was gone for about fifteen minutes before his familiar voice came over the telephone again. As soon as Eunice said "Hello", Walter told her that he loved her very much and that life would have been so much less without her. He went on in this vein for several minutes. The whole thing was a little embarrassing to Eunice. Up until that moment, their conversations had been quite businesslike. After all, those engineers and technicians were all there. Such displays of affection were not usually made in such public surroundings in the 1870's. Eunice recalled later that she thought at the time that the excitement of the forthcoming demonstration had gotten to Walter and he had suddenly gone quite sentimental on her. When Walter stopped talking, Eunice was thankful for the diversion that was offered by the need to start dismantling the set-up and loading it into the car.

Eunice resolved that she was going to have to have a little talk to Walter about his unseemly behavior in that last conversation.

As the engineers were getting the equipment stowed away, Eunice was wondering why it took so long for Walter to get back from around the hill. She knew, however, that he had his own stuff back there to get gathered up and drug back out to the road where they were waiting for him.

About half an hour passed and Walter still didn't show up. The crew was getting a bit impatient so two of the men decided to go out around the hill and help Walter with his gear.

What these two men found left them very thoroughly shaken. They also knew they would have to go back and tell the others. They dreaded that, especially having to tell Eunice that Walter was dead.

The news that these two men had to bring back to the road was that Walter had been attacked and killed by a large and vicious bull out in that pasture. That bull, it was later established, did not belong to the farmer whose pasture they were using. It had apparently broken down a rail fence and had gotten in from a neighboring

pasture. It was determined that the bull had attacked Walter from behind and got him down before the poor man could even run to the safety of a tree.

Those two engineers had additional news they were not sharing with Eunice until they go her back into town to the comfort of her quarters. It was then that the two men told Eunice and the others that the attack had taken place soon after Walter had gone out of sight around the hill on his way toward his equipment. He had not gotten to his equipment, much less had it up. He had never called at all. It was not Walter that had talked to her with those terms of endearment.

That conversation had taken place after the bull had attacked Walter, and killed him. It was the ghost of Walter Hickman that talked to Eunice. It was the ghost of Walter that had shared with her those expressions of his love for her and his appreciation for her.

My research has uncovered other instances in which a ghost's voice was transmitted by the use of a telephone. Certainly, however, Walter's ghost must have been one of the first to use that device which at the time, was the very latest thing in voice communication.

The demonstration across the Niagara River never took place. Nor did, of course, the wedding of Walter Hickman and Eunice.

Eunice did buy the china set in Buffalo. That china is still in the family and reminds the great niece who now owns it of the strange goings-on in that cow pasture southeast of Buffalo, New York in the 1870's.

## CHAPTER II

## THE VIOLIN PLAYER

*A* footbridge was built across the Niagara about two miles below the falls in 1847. This bridge was eight hundred feet long which made it a bit of an ambitious project back in those days. The bridge was a beautiful structure.

The foot bridge immediately attracted the attention of poets and artists. It also attracted a lot of folks who just wanted to view the cascading Niagara Falls from its span.

In 1848, the following year, a young lad had occasion to come to town and was captivated by the bridge. We don't know the lad's name, only that he was endlessly fascinated by that beautiful bridge.

This young country boy was a bit different than most in that he was an accomplished violin player. He was often seen at sunrise out in

the middle of that bridge, softly playing his violin. He played so softly that his music could be heard but slightly, and only when the wind was just right.

This young fellow was a frequent visitor to the bridge during the warm months of both that year and the following. He would show up two or three times a week, and always just after dawn.

It was in August of 1849 when three men doing some repair work on the bridge saw the young fellow with his violin out there in the center, playing to an audience consisting only of the Niagara River.

The later testimony of the three men revealed that the lad had been out there for several minutes. Two of the men happened to be watching him when they saw him trip and fall off of the walkway. They told of how his body fell straight down and the violin slung from his arm, made a huge arc, landing quite a ways from where he did in the water below.

One of the fellows rushed into Niagara Falls to alert the police of the situation while the other two strained their eyes in vain, thinking they might see the young fellow's body from their vantage point high in the air.

Immediately upon learning of the problem, some boats were launched, manned by whoever could be found at the moment, in an effort to locate the boy or his body.

Those efforts, too, were in vain.
There ended up several boats that
were used in the search, and many
men helped, but they found nothing.
Drag lines turned up nothing. A
permanent drag line that had been installed downstream was
checked several times. They didn't find him on that either.

Finally a cannon was put into position and fired out over the water
just upstream from the whirlpool, as well as one downriver by
Niagara-On-The-Lake. It was generally considered, back then, that

firing a cannon out over
the water wouldn't really
cause a body to rise to the
top in spite of some ideas
that it would. It was often
done, however, anyway. It
was easier to do that than
to have to explain why it
wasn't done. The walls of
the Niagara River echoed
back and forth with the booms of those cannons for several hours
before that, too, was given up as unworkable. All these efforts
were to no avail. No body was ever found, nor was the violin.

The incident caused a lot of stir in the area for a few days, but was
soon forgotten until the following summer.

It was that following summer when a fishing party under that
bridge were surprised to hear the melodic strains of a violin early
one morning. Looking up, the fishermen saw the figure of what
appeared to be a young man up on the bridge, playing a violin.

This rather odd situation reminded one of the fellows of the violin player of the previous summer that had fallen from that bridge, and died.

That incident in which the fishermen saw the violin player was repeated several times that summer. It became increasingly obvious that the man up there playing his violin was of the same appearance of the one that had died earlier.

Two young men decided, one day, that this second musician was actually the ghost of the first one. They set out to prove that to be the case, and did a pretty good job of it.

The pair hung around that bridge for several days that summer in hopes of seeing the violin player. The were soon rewarded with just that. One of the two approached him from end of the bridge, and the other from the other end. As the men neared the lone player in the center, he simply disappeared. He just seemed to evaporate, right into thin air.

Subsequent efforts by others, including two law enforcement officers, resulted in the same thing. Many people attempted to get next to the young fellow over the next few years. None could. As the approached, the man would disappear.

The only evidence the fellow ever left that could be found was a violin case. It was lying up there immediately after the ghost of the violin player had put in an appearance.

The records don't reveal to us what happened to that case. Wherever it is, some ghost that played his violin from the bridge across the Niagara River is probably missing it.

## CHAPTER III

## CHAD'S IMAGE

 had and Martha Swanson, like many other newlyweds, were looking forward to seeing the great Niagara Falls on their honeymoon in 1924. Their plans were to go on that honeymoon, then return to their hometown and open up a photography studio. Both of the pair were very interested in photography, and looked forward to having a studio.

An emergency in Chad's family, however, meant that he had to make a quick trip to Minneapolis, Minnesota for a couple of days. Martha therefore, found herself putting away the silver and other nice wedding gifts so that she could travel on to Niagara Falls where she was going to meet Chad the following day.

Martha felt kind of strange, going off to Niagara Falls all by herself on her honeymoon, no less. She knew, though, that Chad would be meeting her there the next afternoon. Neither Martha nor Chad had been to the Falls, so were both really looking forward to seeing that wonder.

Martha was up early the next morning, not having slept well in the strange surroundings of the hotel there in Niagara Falls, New York. She had several hours to while away before Chad arrived, so she thought she would get a head start on her sightseeing of the Falls. Martha had taken several cameras with her since she was an avid photographer as was Chad.

Martha hurried off to Goat Island where she hoped to get some good shots of Horseshoe Falls.

Like everyone else who sees the falls for the first time, Martha was unprepared for the sheer magnitude of what she saw. The sight was unbelievable and the roar from the falls seemed to set the ground to shaking under her feet. Martha almost forget the heavy camera she had drug out there as she stood in open-mouthed amazement of what she saw there from the island.

Martha finally recovered from the breathtaking sight enough to take some pictures of the falls. She was like a kid in a candy store, not knowing which spectacular view to photograph next. She had taken several before she had pointed the camera at the turbulent water at the base of the falls. As she looked through the eyepiece, she was shocked to see her new husband's face clearly formed by the rushing water below. She knew she missed Chad, but felt it was unfair to have to imagine she could see his image in that rushing water.

After snapping that picture, Martha noticed that it was almost eight o'clock, in fact, just five 'til, and that she had planned to be back to the hotel at 8:15 for breakfast. She gathered up her gear and hurried back.

At breakfast, Martha thought again of how she had seen the image of Chad's face in the turbulent water at the base of the falls, and kind of smiled to herself as she realized how much she missed him.

She decided he had better be getting there soon, or she would be imaging all sorts of things. He wasn't due, though, until six o'clock that evening so she decided to do some more sightseeing after breakfast.

So her breakfast was followed by another trip out to see the magnificent falls, as was her dinner that noon. For supper, Martha went back again to the cafe in the hotel. She knew, however, that Chad would be joining her for that so she ordered some flowers to decorate the table.

Martha delayed ordering until Chad was to arrive. She was quite full of this business of being on her honeymoon all by herself and eagerly anticipated his arrival.

The appointed hour came and went, and still no Chad. The pretty flowers had started to lose some of their freshness and she was losing her patience as she kept checking the doorway for her husband to appear.

Her keeping a sharp eye on that door was probably the reason she saw the police officer as soon as he entered the room. She had no reason to consider that he had anything to do with her, of course. She was watching him look around the room as if he were looking for some particular person. Martha was a bit surprised when he caught her eye and came directly to her table. The officer removed his hat and looked at her quietly a moment before he spoke.

The policeman told her of the death of her husband at 7:55 that morning. Martha's world suddenly became one of slow motion. Many images flooded across her mind just before she slipped into unconsciousness. One of those was a recollection of seeing the image of Chad's face in that water at the base of the falls that morning at exactly 7:55, just before going to breakfast.

Martha's next few weeks were a hazy collage of lots of relatives coming to her parents' home to see her, of medication to calm her down and deep grief over the loss of her new husband, Chad. She didn't even know who retrieved her belongings from the hotel or had the photographs developed that she had taken that day.

It was Martha's mother that showed her an odd thing about the photo she had taken at the falls at the moment of Chad's death. The mother and daughter wept together as they looked at that photo and saw Chad's face in the rushing waters of the base of Horseshow Falls.

## CHAPTER IV

## THE HUGE GHOST

aybe this story is about an incident that was really something other than a ghost. But if it wasn't a ghost, it had to be something even stranger. This object was seen in the whirlpool area in 1904. If it was a ghost, it was probably the largest ghost that anyone has ever seen anywhere.

From an account by four men and three children who saw the thing one night in 1904, the thing apparently almost filled the entire gorge where that whirlpool is.

The crowd was out hunting one night There were the three men mentioned above plus two boys that were the sons of one of the men, and another boy, the son of one of the other men.

The records don't tell us how old the children were at the time.

There is conflicting information as to what the men were hunting, but apparently it was a wayward moose.

Their prey led the group that night to the area where the men knew the edge of the cliff was that led down into the whirlpool. The men were being careful not to get too close to the edge, what with the children being along. They sure didn't want to lose a kid over the edge.

As the party neared the edge, they could see something was different. Through the trees they saw what appeared to be a dim light coming up from down in the gorge. Being more curious, now, the group crept all the way to the precipice where they could look down into that area better. All four of the men and the three boys saw the same thing. Almost the entire gorge was filled with a lens-like vaporous object stretching almost from wall to wall. It was thickest in the center. The men estimated it to be a good hundred feet through at that point. The center was also the brightest. The whole thing seemed to give off a soft blue light, but it was most pronounced at the center.

Even as the group watched, they could see that there were lights changing in intensity deep within the center of the object. Two of the fellows had lived in swampy areas and were well aware of what swamp gas looked like. They swore that what they saw that night could not have been swamp gas.

It took several minutes for the men to gather their wits enough to talk to each other. When they did, they compared notes about what they were looking at. They all agreed that they were seeing the same thing.

After about fifteen minutes, the lens-shaped apparition disappeared.

On the anniversary of that event, two of the men and some friends returned to that point overlooking the whirlpool, again at the same time of the night. There was no evidence, that time, of the object.

So was that a ghost? We just don't know. It had the appearance of one, according to the guys who saw in that night in 1904, but that's all we have to go on.

## CHAPTER V

## DRESSED FOR WINTER

**T**his story comes to us from the grandchildren of a man who worked for a short time on the ferry stairway. It was supposed to have taken place around the turn of the century.

The sources of this story don't know if their grandfather's responsibilities involved the operation of the lifting mechanism for the little car, or if he had maintenance or some other duties associated with that famous stairway.

The story goes that this man was off of work, but was a short distance from the base of the structure. The facility was closed and everything was quiet.

Suddenly he heard the distinctive sound of the lift mechanism within the building. He knew that the lift simply would not be operating at that hour of the night. He also knew that if anyone was doing any work on it, he would have been assigned to help.

The man was perplexed about the whole thing. By the time, however, that he had the presence of mind to go to the lower exit to investigate, the car had traveled the entire 330 feet to that point.

As he hurried to the exit he was about one hundred feet away when he saw two women walk out of the building. He was about to hail the pair to find out what was going on when he hesitated over a rather odd thing. It was a warm summer evening, yet these two were all bundled up in cold weather gear. Their heavy coats and caps pulled down for warmth kind of took the fellow off balance for a moment.

All this time, the two women were walking down toward the water with a determined pace as if they knew exactly where they were going and what they were up to.

Those words never did escape the poor fellows lips. By the time he was ready to holler at them this surprising pair had gotten to the water's edge. They just kept right on walking, walking out across the surface of that turbulent river.

With his words stuck in his mouth, our would-be investigator simply watched them walk out of sight in the gathering darkness.

There had been, at the time, some talk about a pair of women ghost who had been seen in that area before. Apparently what the man saw was that pair.

He took it upon himself to look into those stories a bit to see if he could figure out what was going on. He never did shed any light on it all.

# CHAPTER VI

## A SMALL CRY

T he Niagara River has been a part of American life so long that we can only guess at the many secrets buried in its waters and in the soil and rocks of its shores. Many of these are secrets that we will never be told.

Sometimes these secrets are hinted at when an archeologist digs up a long forgotten piece of pottery or a bone. Sometimes as a boy is playing along the edge of the river, he will find, in the mud or rocks, a piece of a flintlock or the stem of an old pipe long discarded or lost by its owner. These chunks of the past are usually flung back into the water, where they sink, and contemplate the ever changing world.

Thus it was in the early 1800's when an unnamed soldier found himself on the west shore of Grand Island. The account that is available doesn't reveal to us what the man was doing on the island, or why he was sitting at the water's edge.
Perhaps he was simply loafing, or fishing. We just don't know.

In any event, he was there looking across the Niagara River when he spotted a relatively large white object that appeared to be twisting and turning as it skirted along the bottom, just under the surface. It was going downstream and was just a couple of feet from the shore.

The man's attention was drawn to the object because of its size, snow-white hue, and its almost hypnotic motion as it passed him on its way down the river.

This odd sight galvanized the soldier to hurriedly find a long stick to snag what he now saw to be a piece of cloth. Even as he grappled for the thing he was again enticed by the movement of it, almost as if it were alive. We have all seen how a piece of cloth will turn and twist in moving water that way.

As the man drug the piece ashore, he could see that it was about two or three foot on a side, and was of a light weight canvas. It was a distinctive cloth, unlike most. The man contemplated it for a moment, for some reason reluctant to throw it back into the river.

In an effort to get a better look at it, the soldier whipped it in the air a couple of times to shake some of the water out of it, then started to twist it in his hands to further wring it out.

Just at that moment he heard a distinct cry. It was of the nature of a cry of pain and seemed to come from behind him. Whirling around, he saw nothing, thinking it must have been to his side. Whirling around, he saw nothing. Thinking it must have been his imagination, he returned to his diversion of wringing that cloth out. Again he heard that cry. This time, the man arose and called out to see who might be near him, but out of sight. Again, nothing. Without even thinking about it, he again begin to twist the cloth as he looked around for the source of that cry. Just as he was doing that, he heard it again. This time was different, however. This time, he could tell where it was coming from. The source of that sound was right there in his own hands. The sound was coming from that cloth!

How could that be? He squeezed the cloth and heard it again, just as if it had come out of the cloth because of his squeezing it.

The account tells of how the soldier dropped the cloth as if it had stung him. It lay there at his feet while he watched it in open-mouth amazement. One last test confirmed his observations. He dropped a rock on it. That brought forth a sound that was all in the world like "Ouch!"

The man backed off and studied the cloth for several moments until he suddenly recalled where he had seen that particular kind of fabric before. He recognized it to be a portion of a burial shroud.

In spite of the series of really odd things that had just happened, the man noticed that there were suddenly a large number of big butter-flies in the air around him. He didn't pay a whole lot of attention to that since there were a whole lot stranger things going on besides a bunch of butterflies.

Somehow, that burial shroud must have been inhabited by the ghost of whoever it had been wrapped around.

The soldier started looking about for the stick he had used to drag the cloth out of the river. He had decided the best thing to do was to poke it back into the river, and get it out of his life. He was going to use that stick for he no longer wanted any part of touching it with his hands.

Then as he was getting ready to do that, he changed his mind and buried the cloth in a shallow grave there on Grand Island. As he explained in his diary, he just didn't have the heart to pitch it back where it might well eventually end up going over the Niagara Falls. His diary entry talked of how he had calculated that if wringing the cloth out was cause enough for pain that the thing would cry out, he didn't want to be responsible for it making that terrible plunge over the falls.

As soon as he completed the job of burying that cloth, another strange thing happened. That bunch of butterflies he hadn't been paying any attention to suddenly all flitted over to the site and rested on the fresh dirt he had filled the hole with. They all faced him, and slowly moved their wings up and down. The soldier had the strong feeling that they were, in some way, thanking him for burying that cloth.

So, perhaps, yet today, 175 years later, there are still some remnants of that cloth in a shallow grave on Grand Island. Or perhaps, it has rotted away, leaving a ghost in the water of the Niagara River or the soil of Grand Island.

## CHAPTER VII

## MISPLACED SOLDIERS

I n 1936 the Grossman couple moved into their new house along that road between Lewiston and Old Fort Niagara.  Well, actually, it wasn't a new house, just new to them.  It was, in fact, an pretty old house.  The Grossmans didn't know how old the building was, nor did any of the neighbors.  That house was simply one of those that outlives peoples' knowledge of their age.  The style of architecture suggested that the house had seen almost a century back in '36 when this story takes place.

The previous owner of the place was obviously very glad to get that old white elephant off his hands. He was having difficulty hiding his glee when they closed the deal. When he gave the Grossmans his assurance that the house was not haunted "in spite of what some of the neighbors might say," that should have tipped the couple off. They thought little of that remark until later, however.

Besides, Mrs. Grossman didn't think such foolishness as "ghost talk" was worthy of her attention, and Mr. Grossman was too busy thinking about how he was going to be able to use the old log shed out in back for raising some chickens and ducks.

The first few nights in the house were uneventful. Those were pretty busy days, getting moved in and all. The Grossmans were enjoying the luxury of having a lot more room than they had where they lived in Buffalo.

Mrs. Grossman had prepared one particular room with a nice view of the Niagara River for a sewing room. It was up on the second floor with several windows for good natural light. She was as anxious to set up a nice sewing room as Mr. Grossman was to get his poultry project going.

She had completely emptied that room up there and had applied a new coat of varnish to the floor.

Being of retirement age, the Grossmans were going to be living in that house alone since their children were all gone by then. Their advancing years made them pretty tired those first few evenings so they went to bed early. The fourth night in the house was no different. They had worked hard and retired at an early hour. It was, in fact, soon after dark, and they had just gotten into bed. As they lay there talking, both of them heard the unmistakable sound of heavy footsteps on the second floor of the house. It wasn't a "maybe" sort of thing. Those steps were clear and distinct.

It was with a certain amount of hesitation that Mr. Grossman climbed those stairs to the second floor to investigate. She busied herself with alternating between urging him to find out what was going on up there and cautioning him to be careful.

Mr. Grossman's investigation up there appeared, at first, to yield nothing. He had, in fact, started back down the steps when he remembered he didn't check that room they had cleared out to re-varnish the floor.

Mr. Grossman retraced his steps down the hall to that room and he looked inside.

For a moment Mr. Grossman had difficulty in believing what he saw. He knew that room was totally free of anything at all. A mouse in the corner would have stood out like a sore thumb in that totally bare room. But it wasn't totally bare when he looked into it. There in the middle of the floor was a pair of what appeared to be very old fashioned leather boots.

 They were high-topped boots of thick cowhide. They even had a silver spur on each of the heels.

No amount of discussion between the two could shed any light on how those boots could have gotten into that room. A pair of boots isn't something a person is apt to overlook when cleaning a floor well, and then re-varnishing it.

The next day the Grossmans showed the boots to some of the neighbors in a shot-in-the-dark attempt to find out who they might belong to.

Nobody knew who they belonged to. One of the neighbors was something of an American history buff and was interested in the boots. He was of the impression that they were some sort of antique military boot. He prevailed upon the Grossmans to let him take the boots to a friend of his in a university who he felt might be able to identify the boots.

Those boots were soon forgotten as the Grossmans encountered one strange thing after another in the house. They saw and heard lots of things for which there was simply no explanation.

Early one morning Mrs. Grossman got up early and caught a glimpse of a pair of what were obviously soldiers walking down the hallway. Speechless, she watched them walk out the front door. No, not out of the doorway, but out of the door. Those two just walked through that solid wood door like it wasn't there. These soldiers didn't have modern uniforms on. She recalled that they looked like some of the old fashioned pictures of soldiers that were in her history book when she was a child.

The Grossmans moved out within a couple of weeks of that incident. That place they moved into didn't have a nice shed out in back for chickens and ducks, but then it didn't have stray soldiers wandering around in it. It had no nice light room for a sewing room, but neither did long dead soldiers leave their old boots laying around.

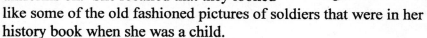

Meanwhile, the word came back from the university that the boots were determined to have been like those worn by Hessian soldiers during the Revolutionary war over a hundred and fifty years earlier.

No one was ever able to figure out why the ghosts of soldiers from so much earlier and so far east were haunting a house in western New York, but that's what they were doing.

The house is gone now, and so undoubtedly, are the misplaced soldiers of Colonial times.

## CHAPTER VIII

## THE UNINVITED GUEST

I n 1905 a man came to Niagara Falls with an odd story. His conversation with the young clerk at the Kaltenbach Hotel was a strange one. He told the clerk that he wanted to stay in the area for a few days and he would be needing a room.

Apparently a gesture by the clerk indicated that a room was available and that he would simply need to register and pay.

The would-be guest, however, told the clerk it wasn't quite as easy as that. He said that he had been haunted all his life by the ghosts of his ancestors and that wherever he went, one or more of these ghosts would follow. He explained that he was quite accustomed to it and that his rather unique problem didn't really bother him any more. He was concerned, however, about the possibility of one of these ghosts would upset some of the other guests. He suggested that perhaps if the hotel had a room somewhat remote from the others, that would minimize the problem.

Such an announcement is not the sort of sort of thing a hotel clerk hears every day, and certainly that one particular clerk hadn't. The befuddled lad stared blankly at his would-be guest, unable to come up with an intelligent response. This simply provided an opportunity for the man to elaborate on his explanation.

"I have been to both THE INTERNA-TIONAL and THE CATARACT HOUSE and explained my problem to them. They both suggested that perhaps a different hotel would be more to my liking."

It isn't known, of course, if the clerks in those two larger hotels were concerned about a ghost, or if the man himself posed a problem to them. After all, how many times does a guest tell a hotel clerk that a ghost will be spending the night there also?

Apparently, the young clerk in the Kaltenbach found neither the would-be guest or the possibility of a ghost for the evening to be a problem, for he recovered his surprise over the situation and motioned to the pen in its holder as if to invite the man to go ahead and register. The man signed, paid the money due, and settled in for the night.

Well, it seems that the man was right about his ancestors. Along about eleven that night, a man dressed in buckskin and what appeared to be a raggedly old buffalo hide came strolling through one of the rooms adjoining that occupied by the haunted man. The occupant of that adjoining room fled his quarters to report to the clerk what he had seen.

That little episode with the buck-skinner was smoothed over by moving the very frightened occupant to another room.

The next complaint wasn't so easily handled. Three doors down the hall from the one occupied by the haunted man was occupied by three ladies of a church delegation attending a convention in Niagara Falls. When, in the middle of the night, a peg-legged man with a lantern came walking through the wall by the bed, clattered across the room on one good leg and a wooden one, then out the other wall. All sorts of carryings-on and complaining ensued. Lady delegates to a church convention are not so easily placated.

The Kaltenback Hotel made some hurry-up arrangements to put their haunted guest up in a nearby rooming house.

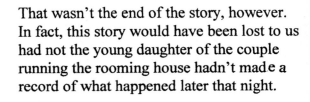

That wasn't the end of the story, however. In fact, this story would have been lost to us had not the young daughter of the couple running the rooming house hadn't made a record of what happened later that night.

After the man was moved to the rooming house, he explained the whole mess to those people. They accepted the fellow anyway and told him they did not care if a ghost came along, just so it didn't disturb their own sleep.

Well, it did just that. The same fellow with the peg-leg showed up in the rooming house along about three in the morning. He was heard thumping his way down the upstairs hallway. The whole family heard the ghost and then saw it. Apparently they didn't even awaken the man to tell him about it. The opportunity to see a ghost made the loss of sleep for the evening a cheap price to pay for that chance.

The daughter's account of the events of that night were written in a journal the next day. That journal is still in the family and rests securely today in a bank vault in Syracuse, New York.

# THE LIBRARY PATRON

T he story of the ghost at the old Carnegie Library at 1022 Main St. in Niagara Falls actually started back in December 10, of 1912. It was on that day that Mrs. Caroline Rank of Watsontown, Pa. visited the library. Mrs. Rank was a frequent visitor to Niagara Falls, and to the library. She stayed with friends while in town. Mrs. Rank was alleged to have been somewhat of an eccentric person, tending to the secretive.

The employees at the library on that December day over three quarters of a century ago had no reason to think that any thing was amiss when Mrs. Rank came for one of her visits. In fact, when they locked up for the night on that day, they were totally unaware that the turn of the key in that front door also locked in the body of Mrs. Rank.

But down in the basement Mrs. Rank's remains were slumped onto the floor as a result of her having shot herself with a 32 caliber hand-gun. In one palm was clutched a note telling that she wanted to be buried in Niagara Falls. It also gave the name and address in Washington, DC. All that was yet unknown, of course to the authorities or the staff at the library.

Things got pretty exciting the following Monday when everybody came back to work at the library. One of the duties of the janitor that day was to clean the auditorium in the base-ment. Armed with the necessary supplies, Mr. Edsall, went down there to do just that.

We can only imagine the shock due Mr. Edsall when he stumbled over the body of Mrs. Rank lying slumped onto the floor there by the piano. Janitors find strange things now and then as they clean and tidy up. The most exciting things that Mr. Edsall was used to finding were things like hidden candy wrappers and secret little notes passed from child to child promising everlasting love. He sure wasn't accustomed to finding bodies in his work there at the library.

Mr. Edsall alerted the library people to his discovery, and the authorities were summoned. The body was moved to the Dykstra morgue on Main St., and things started to get back to normal again.

Things, in fact, got so normal that the suicide in the building was pretty much forgotten. World War I came and went. Lots of changes took place through the years and the memories of the death of an eccentric from out of town just sort of faded. When, almost seventy years later, some strange things begin to happen in the building, no one considered there to be any connection between them and Mrs. Rank. These things were noticed by both the library employees in the building and the people in the Niagara Council of The Arts, Inc. who had worked there. None of those people thought of Mrs. Rank when they would hear footsteps within the building where there should have been none. On occasion, the employees would find doors open that were known to have been shut. The clatter of machines working where there should be none added to the mystery. Most unnerving of all, however, were the feelings that people had that there was an invisible presence in the building that could not be explained.

Most of these incidents were pretty much dismissed by folks in the building for a while. Some, however, felt that an answer to the mysterious happening was at hand when Mr. Donald Loker, a specialist with the library's Local History Department rediscovered an account of the 1912 incident. It was apparent then, that all those goings-on were the work of the ghost of that Mrs. Rank.

Today a tombstone bears the name of Carrie Kerr Ranck - Died Dec. 10, 1912 stands in a Watsontown, Pa. cemetery. It is assumed that the slight change in the spelling of the name is irrelevant, and that the remains of Caroline Rank rest beneath that stone, at least part of the time. An odd detail is that there is no burial record in the cemetery files that that grave is actually occupied.

So is Carrie Ranck the same person as Caroline Rank? If so, is she actually buried there in Watsontown or not? Was it her ghost that came to revisit the site of her death in 1912? Where is her ghost now? We don't know the answers to those questions, of course. We do know that some real strange things happened in that old building at 1022 Main after the death of Mrs. Rank.

* Information for this story courtesy of Local History Dept., Niagara Falls, New York Public Library.

## CHAPTER IX

## THE BROKEN STONE

**W**hen a person thinks of Buffalo, New York, his thoughts will turn to shipping, milling, or manufacturing. One of the last things that most people would associate with Buffalo is the art of diamond cutting. That sort of thing always takes place in New York City, or even some exotic place in Africa or Europe.

But we did have a diamond cutting business in Buffalo in the early 1900's. It wasn't quite as big an operation as the shipping or

milling business, however. It was, in fact, simply a one man operation in the attic of the home of Dr. Baar who lived in a modest house on Clinton Street.

The rumor in the neighborhood was that Dr. Baar had located in Buffalo because he wanted to be far from the main diamond business so he could pursue his work far from the close scrutiny of the law. The rumor went on to say that his business consisted of cutting stolen gems down into smaller and unrecognizable shapes.

There is no evidence that Dr. Baar was running any such illegal operation, but stories like that do get started. We do know, however, that he was in the practice of re-cutting gems to clean them up of chips and to eliminate flaws.

The source of this story told me about what happened when Dr. Baar cut one particular diamond down into two smaller ones.

The stone in question was a rather large diamond that Dr. Baar had gotten from the executor of what had been a large estate in Syracuse. Apparently the surviving wife had lost a lot of her wealth while she was yet alive. Her death precipitated a legal battle among her heirs that just about devoured the rest of it.

The diamond ring that Dr. Baar had agreed to re-cut was just about the end of what had been appreciable holdings. The stone had a tiny flaw that could be eliminated by re-cutting. The elimination of that flaw would increase the total value well beyond Dr. Baar's fee, so it was to have been well worth the cost.

This particular diamond was still mounted in its luxuriously ornate gold ring. The ring was that given by the late husband of the woman on the occasion of their marriage. In tiny, tiny letters, and decorated with hearts and flowers was the inscription "My Love Will Endure As This Diamond."

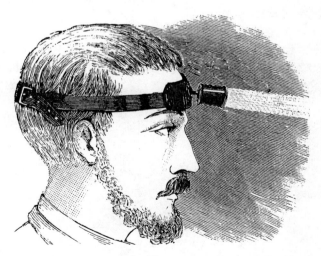

Dr. Baar studied that inscription before removing the stone from its setting. Obviously the woman's husband meant, in that inscription, that his love would last forever, thinking that the diamond would also. Dr. Baar thought it ironic and a little sad that the inscription would allude to the timelessness of the diamond, and there he was preparing to split it in half. He momentarily felt bad about what he was getting ready to do.

"No matter!", he thought. "Both of those people are dead now and my job is simply to rework this stone. An inscription from one person to another is meaningless now that they are both gone."

The diamond splitting business is touchy. A notch is ground into the stone, then a steel blade is inserted into the notch. The blade is

then struck with a wooden mallet. If everything goes alright, the diamond will split along the line of that notch.

Dr. Baar studied the stone for several days, making a variety of measurements in order to assure himself that when he brought that mallet down, it would split where it was supposed to. By the time he would be ready, he'd make that notch where he knew it should be.

Dr. Baar's first surprise came when he brought that stone up against the cutting wheel to make the notch. The diamond no sooner touched the wheel when he heard a loud and angry voice.

"No, No! Don't touch that diamond!"

That, of course, really took Dr. Baar by surprise since he was alone in the house and he knew he had locked the door at the base of the

stairs before he had started to work on that job. He turned the machine off and looked around him for the owner of that voice. The stairway behind him, leading down to the first floor was empty. Repeated searching of the room also yielded nothing. He was totally alone, yet he knew he had heard that voice.

A rather shaken Dr. Baar finally returned to his table, totally confused as to where that angry command might have come from.

As if to chase the experience from his mind, he picked up the blade and set it against the stone. With a quick tapping motion, he drove that blade into the diamond, splitting it into two parts.

There probably hadn't been a woman in that building for the previous twenty years. Dr. Baar was unmarried and was all but a recluse. When a loud woman's sob filled the room as that diamond fell into its two parts, Dr. Baar knew then what had happened. The ghosts of the woman and her husband inhabited that diamond and had protested his splitting it - he with his angry outburst and she with a sob.

As Dr. Baar stood there, realizing that his splitting the diamond somehow violated the bond between the coupled, he knew he had made a mistake in taking on that job.

With a rush of sadness, he also suddenly knew that that violation made even more painful his own lack of human warmth. For the first time in his life he deeply regretted not having married and having a family of his own. Suddenly he felt compelled to do what he could to undo what he had done even as he stood there thinking that over, the two portions of the stone seemed to vibrate and draw closer together. They rolled, on that level table top, until once again, they lay side by side.

Dr. Baar covered the stones and his equipment with a dust cloth and composed a letter to the executor of the estate. He told, in his letter, that he would continue the work only if he could be assured that the stones would be remounted into a single setting rather than in separate ones. He also told the executor that he would do that and wanted to inscribe a phrase on the ring much like that that was on the original.

In addition, he suggested to the executor that if he would agree to all that, he would not charge for his services.

So that's what was done. Somewhere in Buffalo or Syracuse is a beautiful ring today, set with two diamonds and a brand new inscription that says:

"OUR LOVE WILL ENDURE AS THESE
DIAMONDS"

## CHAPTER X

### AVERY'S GHOST

his story started at 6:30 in the morning of a July day one hundred and forty four years ago. It was a day of drama and a day of tragedy at Niagara Falls.

It started that morning with the discovery, by an early riser, of a man clinging to a log that had become entrapped in the rocks of the rapids just above the precipice and below the bridge to Goat Island.

News of the man's situation quickly spread throughout the community and thousands of people witnessed the several attempts made to save the poor fellow. It was generally considered that the job was all but done when a crew of men managed to slowly play out some rope so as to lower a boat from below the bridge to the man. The boat approached the fellow to the cheers of the onlookers.

It turned out that things weren't going to be that easy, however.

The rope holding the boat became entangled up under the same log to which the man clung.

The would-be rescuers found they couldn't pull the thing back again. The same fate awaited the raft that they lowered after the boat. By that time, of course, the area by that log was getting crowded with stuff they couldn't drag back to the bridge.

Undaunted, the men lowered another boat. That one had the rope fixed in such a manner as to prevent it from fouling with the rocks or the log. The crowd even started to drift away, knowing the operation was all but over. The victim, Joseph Avery, had gotten up on the raft, standing there waiting for the boat being eased down to him. The fellows on the bridge let it come too fast. It slammed onto the raft, throwing Joseph off and over the edge. Repeated efforts to find his body were no more successful than those spent in trying to save his life.

The episode took place over a rather prolonged period of time and was witnessed by many people, so Joseph Avery became one of the best known of the victims of the falls.

That wasn't the end of the case. It was three years later when interest in the Joseph Avery tragedy revived.

It all started in a tavern in Niagara Falls. The fellows were all more or less minding their own business when a man entered the

room. All eyes immediately fell on him, for his appearance was unlike what the folks were used to. His skin was pure white except for around his eyes. There was almost black skin surrounding two of the most piercing eyes any of the fellows had ever seen. His clothes consisted of a simple black hooded cape that extended all the way to the floor.

More than one of the fellows looked at the figure standing in the door and wiped their eyes in hopes of clearing their vision. Certainly that was an odd and evil looking man standing there. One of the guys said it was as if the man was devouring the room with those eyes.

The silence that followed the appearance of the hooded man was broken by the appearance of a short and pudgy little guy all decked out in a suit, complete with diamond cuff links and a flowered lapel. He squeezed in from behind the tall hooded character and led him into the room with a hand on his companions' arm.

The pudgy little fellow announced to the still-stunned occupants of the room that his tall friend was the ghost of the Joseph Avery who had died in his fall into the falls three years earlier.

"Yes, folks," he said, "This is the ghost of poor Joseph Avery. He appeared to me, and I am arranging for Joseph here to tell you about his horrible death in 1866. Joseph will address an audience in three days from tonight at Prospect Park."

The little guy filled the total silence that followed his announcement with more details about Joseph and how he was going to tell the folks about how it was to go over the edge of the falls.

Meanwhile the barkeep stood as if transfixed over the whole affair.

Almost seeming as if to ignore the shock his words brought to his audience, the pudgy little guy kept at it just like he was a barker in a circus.

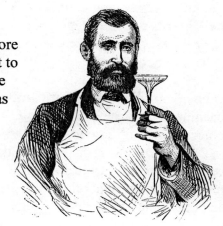

"After all, folks, who among you have had an opportunity to hear of such a tale? How many of you have been told how it is to die by someone who has actually done it?"

He went on to tell the boys there at the bar what time the speech would be and the cost of the tickets for admission.

Well, all this caused quite a bit of a stir, of course. There were those who believed, and there were those who claimed the whole thing was just a hoax.

Avery's ghost said almost nothing during the next day or two as his pudgy little sidekick showed him off around town, promoting the speech that his tall and quiet friend was going to be giving at the park soon.

The police were called in on the case, but apparently no one could think of any specific law that was being violated. After all, ghosts weren't illegal, nor was it against the law for one of them to go on the lecture circuit.

The excitement of the affair built with the approaching hour of the presentation. There is no record of how many tickets were sold or what they cost. Apparently, the promise of hearing from Joseph Avery himself about his death was providing to be a lucrative business for the oddly matched couple putting the whole thing together.

There was also, of course, an ongoing controversy raging along as to whether or not the ghost was a hoax. This reached a peak on the day before the GREAT JOSEPH AVERY SPEECH was to be given.

On that day before the speech a man came into town with the announcement that he was the cousin of the departed Joseph Avery, and wanted to question this so-called ghost.

With a lot of noise and fanfare, a meeting between the ghost and the cousin was arranged. With a very obviously display of skepticism, the cousin challenged the ghost to answer some questions about Joseph Avery. The cousin asked such things as Joseph's nickname when he was a child, the birth date of his mother, his father's middle name, etc. These were questions whose answers would not be known to an imposter. The confrontation was attended by as many that could squeeze into the room.

The ghost answered all the questions without hesitation or error, so it became apparent to all those witnessing the exchange that this was indeed none other than the ghost of Joseph Avery.

At the end of the meeting of the ghost and the cousin, the cousin tearfully embraced the ghost, the pudgy little fellow, and two girls down at the end of the bar. He left the place assuring everybody that he had been wrong in his suspicion. That was the ghost of Joseph Avery, no doubt about it.

The cousin then left Niagara Falls, rather quickly, some of the few remaining disbelievers, noted.

That little exchange with the cousin was all it took to send ticket sales up and up. The forthcoming speech became the subject in every conversation.

The whole thing would have come off nicely, except for an observation made by an actor who was visiting the falls. He made the comment that the ghost sure looked like he was all made up with cosmetics.

He said "I'll bet that white face is actually powder, and the blackness around his eyes is grease."

Well, that set off all kinds of new speculation among the folks. The whole thing fell apart soon after that. A particularly gutsy young man of about sixteen edged up to the "ghost" with a handkerchief.

Fortunately for the youth, he guessed right. His handkerchief came away smeared with the powder and grease of stage makeup.

Somehow, in the next couple of hours, the     pair made good their escape, getting away with both their hides and the receipts from all those ticket sales.

Needless to say, there was no ghost speech in Prospect Park.

Several of the victims of the scam vowed to find that pair of scoundrels as well as the "cousin" who led them astray. Apparently, no one ever did.

After I heard this story I couldn't help but think of what would happen if Avery's real ghost ever did show up in Niagara Falls. He'd probably have a tough time getting believed.

# CHAPTER XI

## THE WOODCUTTER

The Ben Nielson family south of Tonawanda had a strange situation at their home. Most of it happened during a five day period in November of 1936.

It all started when the Nielsons found one of their trees at the edge of the yard chopped down. Ben's first impulse was to blame the oldest boy, Wilt. Wilt loved to play with an axe so was a logical suspect. As Ben examined the stump, however, he realized that Wilt had neither the skill  nor the strength to make those large clean chips. He knew it had to be someone better with an ax, than was Wilt.

So, who would have done that, and why, was a total mystery to Ben Nielson. There were more than enough trees around that no one would have had reason to try to steal one so close to a house.

Ben didn't have long to wait for the mystery to deepen. Two days later when he woke up one morning, he found another tree lying at the edge of the clearing. That one, too, had been cut by someone who knew what they were doing. It wasn't the work of a kid.

Now this was getting to be too much. Someone was cutting his trees down, and doing so right there near the house! Ben resolved to catch the culprit and teach him a lesson about messing with other people's property.

His scheme was to sleep on that side of the house with the window open so he could hear everything going on outside. His strategy got him nothing but a head cold, sleeping by that open window in November. The next morning saw the third and fourth trees lying on the grown, one of them already having been reduced to firewood.

This was going too far! It was enough to have some-body cutting the trees down there at the edge of his yard, but to do so while escaping detection was too much. Chopping a tree down is not the most quiet operation, yet somehow, the guy was getting away with it.

Ben knew he was going to have to do whatever was necessary to catch the guy. So that night he moved a chair over to the bedroom window, and turned off the lights.

That procedure paid off. Along about three in the morning a slumbering Ben Nielson was jerked awake by his dog growling and looking toward the window as if he heard something outside. Ben looked out of that window and saw a figure in work clothes coming out of the timber into the clearing surrounding the house. On the man's shoulder was a

double bitted axe. Without hesitation, the intruder selected a tree and began to chop.

Ben Nielson could hardly believe the fellow would have that much nerve, but there the evidence was, right in front of him.

Ben walked out to the man in such a way that he got almost to him before being seen. He just started to holler at him when the man whirled around and glared at Ben just as if Ben were the intruder instead of the other way around.

Then, without a word, he changed right before Ben's eyes. He seemed to become formless, like a column of smoke, then just disappeared. All that was left was an axe that clattered to the ground and one very very surprised Ben Nielson.

Ben learned from a neighbor several days later what was going on. It seems that Ben hadn't been the only occupant of that house that had been bothered by the ghost woodcutter. Among the previous residents, were several others who had seen the ghost woodcutter. One of them had known the original settler in person and had recognized the ghost as being the ghost of that first settler; an Irishman by the name of Sean Kelly.

The theory in the neighborhood was that old Sean Kelly had worked so hard at clearing that building site, he just hadn't bothered to quit when he died. Apparently, through the years the clearing had grown considerably as that ghost did his work.

After that rash of cutting trees near Ben's house ran its course, Old Sean Kelly showed up only on rare occasions. Ben could just about count on losing a tree now and then, however. He took the attitude that Sean could do as he wanted so long as he didn't get too carried away with it. So Sean and Ben sort of established a relationship that lasted a good many years.

It's been several years now since Sean had done his thing at the house. Ben is gone now, too. The new owners have heard about a ghost on the place but have never seen or heard one.

# CHAPTER XII

## A SHELL OF A MAN

he story of the stranger at Pete's Blacksmith Shop outside of Cheektowaga is one I got from the grandson of Pete himself.

The incident was supposed to have taken place either in 1902 or 1903 right there in Pete's shop.

It was on a fall afternoon and Ed Shaun was there at Pete's getting a wheel rim mounted on a buggy wheel. Pete's cousin, Wilber Hoffman, was also in the shop, loafing more than anything else.

The boys were settin' around talking about whatever when a stranger appeared at the door with a single-tree he wanted straightened.

The new fellow just seemed to kind of fit right in, talking about how he thought the forthcoming winter was going to be, prices of things, and hunting, of course. Both Ed and Wilber took a liking to the stranger, Pete, bein' too busy to do much visiting.

The stranger never did reveal his name to the boys, and they didn't ask. Sometimes when a fellow will fail to tell his name, that's all there is to it. Other times, it is because there seems to be an unspoken agreement not to talk about it. That was the way it was with the stranger.

The wheel rim that Ed had brought was the thing that caused a series of events that made this tale.

Apparently the rim was a large one and clumsy to handle because Ed was helping Pete lift and turn it. The thing caught on the end of a heavy crowbar stored overhead in the ceiling joists. That bar came crashing down, hitting the stranger on the head, and then burying its pointed end in the man's left arm.

Pete, Ed, and Wilber all raced over to the poor fellow laying there on the floor, not moving a muscle. With a grit of his teeth, Pete pulled that iron bar out of the stranger's arm. Pete expected, of course, to see lots of blood from that severe puncture.

Tearing off the shirtsleeve of the unconscious man, Pete was shocked to see that there was no blood around the puncture at all. Without thinking, Pete put his hand on the wound to try to understand why the man was not bleeding.

As Pete touched the man's arm, a fragment of papier' maiche-like piece of what Pete had thought was skin broke off under Pete's hand and fell into the hollow arm. All three fellows could look down into an empty shell-like arm. There was no flesh, no bone, no nothing in there. It was just like a thick egg shell.

All this, of course, caused the fellows to stand up and to take a new look at the stranger.

As the man laid there with his head thrown back and his mouth open, the boys discovered another thing. They found they could see that while the outside of his head looked normal, there was no inside to it. They could see he had nothing in there. There was no roof to his mouth and the whole head was as empty as a bucket The boys could see the curve of the back of his head through his mouth. It appeared as if his head was made of the same papier' mache as was his arm. They all realized at the same time this was an odd fellow, for sure.

All talk of weather and hunting took a back seat to this new situation. The boys had talked with this guy and had no idea that there was anything amiss. Yet it was now clear that he wasn't a normal person at all, maybe he wasn't a person at all!

Ed suddenly decided he had something important to do at home, so he took off with a hurried "good-bye".

Pete, meanwhile, speculated that thing was a lot bigger than he was, and he had better go for the sheriff. He told Wilber to watch the shop and he'd be right back.

So Wilber found himself with that carcass, or whatever it was. He wasn't very comfortable with the situation, but figured he would have to put up with it until Pete got back with the Sheriff.

Wilber's account of what happened next cannot be collaborated, of course, since he was alone. He claimed, however, that a few minutes after Pete left, he went to check the body and it was gone.

The three fellows got together later and speculated for a long time over what could possibly be an explanation for what had happened that afternoon. The only thing they could think of was that the stranger was a ghost.

When other people would scoff at that theory, they would ask just what was it then. No one had a better idea. Neither do I.

## CHAPTER XIII

## THE PAMPHLET

 echnically, this is a ghost story appropriate for a book of ghost stories about the Nagara River because it is about a ghost and it happen within sight of the Niagara River, in Buffalo.

The people involved were, however, New York City people who came to Buffalo under protest, stayed with the same attitude, and then left within hours after circumstances allowed them to.

The story started in New York City with the odd behavior of a woman living there.

Mrs. Tostal was the only daughter of a strong willed, tyrannical, and extremely wealthy man who provided for her and Mr. Tostal.

Mr. Tostal found it unnecessary to work since his father-in-law gave the couple whatever they might need, and a lot of what they wanted.

Mrs. Tostal didn't work either, of course. It was in the late 1800's and ladies of genteel breeding simply didn't stoop to such things. She was busy, however. She put in long days in the basement of their home in New York City printing leaflets exposing her favorite political or social causes.

She would print these pamphlets by the hundreds and then carefully put each in an envelope before loading them all on her bicycle

to deliver to the folks up and down the streets within a few blocks of their home.

Everybody knew she was a couple of bricks shy of a load. Not that promoting causes is odd, but her choice of causes was bizarre. One of her favorites was about fish. She would expound endlessly about the fish, making impassioned pleas for something or other. No one could every really figure out what she was trying to convince people of.

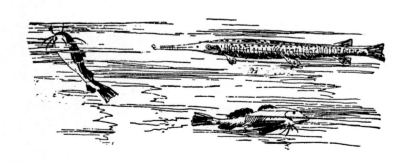

Mrs. Tostal's behavior grew steadily worse and worse. Her pamphlets became less and less comprehensible. Her father's impatience with that foolishness grew as her eccentricity did.

He, unfortunately, one day saw her latest issue of the pamphlet. The entire thing was nothing but 5's. There were big 5's, and little ones. There were plain ones and fancy ones but they were all 5's, nothing else. She had been delivering that issue just as she had previous ones.

When her father saw that one, it was the last straw. He served notice on his daughter and her husband that they were to leave the city and to live elsewhere until she straightened herself out. The couple was given the choice of any of several cities where they could go, and where he would set them up with a nice home and all they would need.

Why Buffalo was chosen, no one knows. But it was. The couple came to town, bought a large and beautiful home overlooking the river, and settled down. Settling down for him meant puttering in his library and in his garden. Settling down, for her, meant getting her printing machine set up so she could get her pamphlet out again.

Since the Tostals never really acknowledged the presence of the city of Buffalo, they rarely ventured from the house. They apparently thought they were camping out, being that far from New York City.

Not leaving the house didn't slow Mrs. Tostal down. After all, there were lots of people who needed to see her pamphlets; her husband for one. Then there were the servants and the gardener.

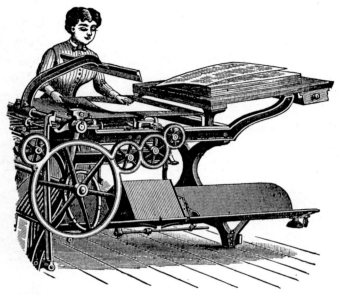

Several times a week delivery people and repairmen would have reason to come to the house. These were all "clients" also. All these people needed her pamphlet, and she wasn't about to let them down. As in her home in New York City, she would deliver the pamphlet to her unwilling "clients" by making her rounds of the halls and grounds on her bicycle.

Apparently, being out of sight was as good as being out of mind for her father. He kept them supplied with money and told them the money would keep coming as long as they stayed in Buffalo.

After several years in their new home, Mrs. Tostal died. Since she was the reason they had to live in Buffalo, that event enabled him to move back to New York City. The house stood empty for many years, steadily falling into a state of ruin due to neglect.

The Tostal home eventually became a total wreck with stray cats on the first floor and squirrels on the second.

The frequent noises coming from that old hulk of a house from those playful little squirrels and the cats chasing each other started to attract the attention of the neighborhood children. They knew, of course, that those noises weren't cats and squirrels. They knew those were noises from ghosts.

So the house soon developed a reputation as a haunted one. Each strange noise generated a story which then, in turn, added to the legends about the place. It wasn't too long before every kid in the neighborhood was firmly convinced the house was chuck full of spooks.

None of the neighboring adults believed there were ghosts in the old Tostal house. That is, none of them did until 1896 when several men entered the house to study what could be salvaged. They had contracted with the owner to get the thing torn down. Apparently, there were plans to erect a new building in that place.

The fellows were upstairs when they heard the clank-clank-clank of a machine operating. This came as a bit of a surprise, of course. They hadn't expected to find any sign of human life in that old wreck, much less anyone operating a machine of some sort.

Following the sound of that machine, the men found themselves in a small room on the second floor watching a woman cranking out copies of a small pamphlet.

The lady looked at the group of fellows, held a handful of pamphlets toward them, and then with a smile, she walked on out through the wall.

Finding a woman putting out pamphlets in that vacant house left the fellows pretty shocked, But when she walked out through the wall, that was something else! It took a few moments for the guys to get their wits gathered enough to rush to the windows to look out to try to find out how she did that.

It was several minutes until one of the fellows took the time to look at the pamphlets lying around on and around the machine. It was a nice and clean printing job. The characters were crisp and the whole job looked good.

The contents of the pamphlets were totally incomprehensible, however. It was just a string of words, fragments of words, and numbers. There seemed to be something about fish in the thing, but nobody would fathom what it was all about. Not at first, anyway. Soon, however, one of the fellows recalled years earlier when he had been a delivery boy for a local grocery store. he again remembered those pamphlets he kept getting when he went to one of the fancy houses overlooking the river. Memories of those strange pamphlets and the strange woman who printed them reminded him of where he had seen that woman before.

This now-adult delivery boy told the other fellows of the Tostal home and the odd going-on there. he told the guys that what they had seen was a ghost - the ghost of Mrs. Tostal.

# CHAPTER XIV

## THE HEIRLOOMS

**T**he Harter family had no reason to think their home was haunted when they lived on the south edge of Buffalo back in the early 1920's. They hadn't heard any noises, seen anything strange or had things disappear or fly across the room.

The Harters were not wealthy by the standard of the time, but they were comfortable, and enjoyed all the life's necessities, and many of its luxuries. Mrs. Harter had received a tidy inheritance which the couple invested and pretty much lived from the proceeds.

In addition to the cash that Mrs. Harter had gotten, she had also been given several family heirlooms such as furniture, a couple of nice oil paintings and a beautiful piece of marble statuary. Both the paintings and the stature portrayed earlier family member.

One of the paintings showed Mrs. Harter's great-grand-parents. The other was of her grandfather as a child. That same great-grandmother in the painting was represented by the statue. The Harter children often enjoyed study-ing the similarity of their great-great-grandmother in the painting with the statue, even down to a small blemish on the right side of her face near her lip.

It was well after the children grew up when Mrs. Harter died. Relatives all gathered for the funeral, of course. All three of the children came home for the occasion.

By this time, the Harter children had families of their own. The oldest of these three children, Albert, was in the house showing his daughter, Amy, the various rooms and how he had grown up there with his two sisters. It was a bit of an exercise in nostalgia for the man. It had been a good home and Albert was anxious to share, with Amy, what his childhood had been like.

When the pair got to the parlor, it was just a matter of moments before they found themselves standing in front of those oil paintings. They were more or less, the focal point of the room, and two of the things that he remembered best.

Albert started to explain to Amy how he and his sisters had so often played in that room and how they had so enjoyed studying those relatives in the paintings. Suddenly he stopped talking and stared intently at the paintings of his great-great-grandparent.

"What's wrong, Daddy?"

"Why, nothing, Amy. I just didn't remember that those two had tears in there eyes. I sure don't remember that."

Then with a little laugh, Albert hugged his daughter and said:

"I know why I hadn't seen those tears before. Look, when I lean way down like this, I'm farther away and can't see them. When I was a kid, I would have been way down here. I'm taller now, and up where I can see them better."

A call for lunch interrupted the tour, so Albert and Amy left the room, deciding to come back later.

It was later that evening when Albert remembered what he had discovered tears in that portrait. All of a sudden, he couldn't wait to tell his

to tell his
about that.
to believe it.
however, that
tears didn't
he leaned way
he would have
was a child.

two sisters
They refused
He explained,
he found the
show up when
down where
been when he

"They don't
clear, so we
missed them
down where
looking."

show up real
would have
from way
we were

One of the girls
believe him, so
crowd had to go
settle the issue.

still didn't
the whole
to the parlor to

Sure enough, the girls saw those tears also. The group was standing there telling each other how remarkable it was that they hadn't seen that as children, but could then understand how that could have been.

Some of the party had already started to drift for the door to return to another room when Amy called for everybody to look at the statue of her great-great-grandmother.

"Look here. She's crying here in the statue too."

That, of course, was impossible. Those portraits might have seemed a mile away to a small child in that high-ceilinged room, but the statue was something else. The statue had always been on a pedestal near the piano where the kids could have always reached it without difficulty. In fact, it still bore the evidence of those soiled fingers that had thoroughly explored every detail of the woman's face. Not even the slightest feature had escaped the scrutiny of the three children when they were little.

Amy's announcement brought everyone to the pedestal. There, streaming down both of the statue's cheeks, were tears frozen in marble.

The noisy babble of the littlest children in the crowd grew silent as they realized that all the adults were not saying a word. Each eye on the statue was misty as each of the adults understood what was going on. Those tears were just as obvious as they could be, yet they hadn't been there before.

Albert was the first to speak.

"I was wrong. The reason we hadn't seen the tears in the paintings when we were kids is because they weren't there. Those tears are new and these tears are new. Mother's great-grandparents are not simply images on canvas and a hunk of marble. They are sharing with us today, our grief over the loss of our mother."

Today, each of the three Harter have an heirloom in their homes that reminds them of how earlier members of their family had crossed the bridge of time to share in the loss of a loved one.

## CHAPTER XV
## BUD IN THE SNOW

**T**his is an account of a series of events that was supposed to have taken place in a cemetery in an older section of Buffalo. It was said to have been not too far off of what was known as Lockport Road. If this was the same Lockport Road that we know of today, we just don't know.

The name of the principal player in this is was alleged to be "Bud". We don't know if this was his first name, his last name, or even if it might have been a nickname. It gets kind of "iffy" to attempt to find a "Bud" in the cemetery records.

In any event, this Bud fellow was alleged to have been a resident of Buffalo, and while alive to have a huge aversion to snow. One wonders why Bud even lived in the area. Living in Buffalo and really hating snow seems like a strange way to go. One wonders why the man didn't simply move somewhere else. Buffalo gets more than enough snow for someone who likes the stuff, and just one heck of a lot more than one can handle if he hates it.

But, that was apparently the situation, a guy living in Buffalo who hated snow. This fellow was apparently obsessed with his dislike for that powdery stuff. He refused to go out in it. He refused to shovel it and would even get angry with his family if they talked about snow.

It was reported that he bought his house in the summer time. He was supposed to have broken up the sidewalk into the house, and replaced it with new concrete in which he had embedded electric wires, so he could throw a switch inside and heat the sidewalk up so the snow would melt off rather than to be faced with the need to go out into it to shovel his walk.

It is also reported that he did the same thing with the driveway so he could melt the snow off of the driveway from the comfort and safety of his home.

Bud was supposed to have lived in Buffalo back in the early 1920's. Back then, most homes didn't even have cement driveways, much less one with electric wires in it to melt snow off of the thing.

Apparently, there was no such thing as too much trouble or too much cost to get around the need to shovel snow.

The fellow telling me this story was the son of Bud's neighbor, and told of how his father had often remarked at how odd it was that Bud went to all that trouble. Apparently hiring some kid to shovel that snow off wasn't good enough for Bud.

In due course Bud joined his ancestors, and passed on to his just rewards. We can guess that his concept of Heaven would be a place where it never snowed.

Wherever Bud was scheduled to go after death, he apparently never made the trip. It appears that he hung right in there at his gravesite to see to its proper maintenance.

"Proper maintenance" for Bud's gravesite apparently meant . . . . . . "kept free of snow."

Bud was supposed to have shucked these mortal coils in late May, so he was buried then, and nothing of note happened at his grave site for several months.

But, come the first snow that November, that things started perking around Bud's gravesite.

The first observation that something odd was afloat was when a maintenance man at the cemetery during that November made a strange observation. He noticed that the light skiff of snow that had come in the night pretty much laid all over the cemetery . . . . that is all over the cemetery except for a three by eight foot section in front of Bud's tombstone. It was that three by eight foot section that laid directly above the casket holding the mortal remains of our Bud.

While that situation seemed a bit odd to that maintenance man, he didn't think a whole lot about it. Sometimes when soil is disturbed as it was to allow the burial of the casket, the soil will hold or release water differently simply because it was disturbed and is thereby different from the surrounding soil.

That maintenance man had worked in a cemetery enough years that he knew that, and wasn't particularly moved by the fact that snow apparently hadn't stayed in that three by eight foot area as long as it had elsewhere in the cemetery. He had, in fact, all but forgotten that situation by the time a heavier snow came that lasted all night. By morning, the cemetery has been changed to a sea of whiteness. That is, it had been, except for a three by eight foot section directly in front of Bud's gravestone.

That snow was a good six or eight-inches deep that morning all over, except that one spot, of course.

Now the physical properties of soil may change a bit as a result of digging it up and putting it back, but not nearly enough to cause such as thing as that on that cold cold November morning.

Reporting of the situation to the maintenance man's boss, pretty much put the whole mystery to rest. The man's boss knew about Bud's aversion to snow, and told his worker that Bud's widow must have come out really early that morning to shovel off the grave in remembrance of her recently departed husband.

The boss, in fact, saw Bud's widow later that week downtown, and remarked at how she must have really gotten up early that morning to clear the snow from her husband's gravesite.

The man couldn't really understand why the woman denied having done that. He just figured that she was still handling her grief over losing Bud, and didn't want to talk about it all.

That first good snow didn't disappear by the time the next one came. It came during the day, ending in the late afternoon just before it got dark.

Glancing out the window, the boss who had such a ready answer for the bald spot in the cemetery before, was surprised to see the additional snow that came that afternoon covered the entire cemetery . . . . well, almost the entire cemetery. The reader can guess what three by eight foot section was totally free of any snow, showing the brown soil in stark contrast all all the white everywhere else.

Now, all of us know that old man winter is not a respecter of persons, and we know that snow must have fallen on that gravesite.

And, we are left with the only reasonable explanation of those vents. It must have been the ghost of Bud who saw to the removal of that snow as soon as it landed.

If a mortal man can engineer the automatic removal of snow with the flip of a switch from a living room, his ghost must have figured some was to manage a little three by eight foot section of a cemetery.

The fellow telling me about the situation went on to tell of how the whole issue became a real mystery. He told of how the cemetery people and some of Bud's family had several get-togethers over the whole thing. He told of how the family posted a watch over the gravesite when snow was predicted. Apparently nothing of interest came out of that little experiment, and the whole issue soon faded away.

Unfortunately, my source of information didn't know if interest in the issue faded away because folks simply accepted these strange events, or if they lost interest.

So, today, we are left with the situation in which either nothing of interest is happening with that gravesite, or folks are no long noticing.

In a better world, we would know which cemetery it was and what Bud's real name was so we could check it all out. But, we don't know that, so we're stuck with just this story out of the past.

# CHAPTER XVI

## ROSIE'S ROSES

T his account, like the previous one is a story out of a cemetery.

It would be fun to know that this story is about the widow of Bud from the previous story, since it has some elements in common with the Bud Story.

Unfortunately, we have no information that would suggest this is a story about Bud's widow.

In fact, I'd guess it couldn't have been since this is a story about events in a cemetery on Grand Island. We don't know much about the occupant of the gravesite in that cemetery on Grand Island except the occupant's name was Rose Mc-Donald. I kind of wish the woman's name hadn't been Rose since the story has to do with roses, and her bearing that name is just too coincidental. I'd be tempted to say this story was a fake, but it was told to me as being a true story, so I'm reporting it as such in this book.

The events of this story start out, like the previous one, about the likes and dislikes of a person before she died.

Rose's little quirk was that she was an avid gardener, and that the bulk of her garden was devoted to . . . of all things . . . rose plants.

I guess we can't fault a woman by the name of Rose for really liking roses. It is, as I say, just a tad bit too coincidental to me.

But, anyway, Rose did her thing with roses. Not only did she devote most of her garden to roses, but she also used a lot of them in decorating her home. She was supposed to have a fresh bouquet of roses on her dining room table the entire season they were in bloom.

Apparently, she was rather good at raising roses because she was well known in the neighborhood for her beautiful garden and the lovely floral arrangements she had in the house, all either dominated by roses, or used only roses.

Like many practitioners of hobbies, she ran the whole thing in the ground. She got in the practice of making a rose petal based tea, using her roses for dried arrangements, ground 'em up to put in her homemade soap, etc.

She loved her roses, and just kind of overdid the whole thing.

Rose's love of roses would ordinarily have been soon forgotten by most everybody. Our hobbies we are so interested in have a way of getting shuffled off into forgotten corners after we die.

Undoubtedly Rose had neighbors who where into making quilts, preparing prize winning pickles or some other such thing. Those quilts, pickles or whatever are now lost to time, but the story of Rose's roses lives on.

Again, like most ghost stories, it all started when it ended, that is when Rose died.

Roses death was not anymore or less remarkable than any one of many other housewives deaths. Her funeral was apparently of little lasting note. After the funeral, things got put away, and there was nothing to suggest that Rose was going to be heard from again.

But, she was. At least those of her friends and relatives who know of this story, are convinced that Rose pretty much hung around, even after she left.

For a few years, relatives would bring flowers to Rose's grave on Memorial Day. Back then, they called it Decoration Day, but the effect was the same. Folks would take flowers to gravesites, sort of tidy up around them, and then pretty much disappear until a year later.

Since it was family that would
"do" Rose's grave on Decoration
Day, they usually took roses to
adorn the gravesite, all of them
recalling how much she likes
that beautiful flower.

Those roses gave way, eventually
to artificial flowers, and finally to
very infrequent visits.

The real mystery of this story
happened in 1953 when some of
the local church ladies decided to plant flowers along the drive
up through the cemetery, and near the headstones of some of the
graves that never seemed to get visited anymore.

Rose's gravesite was one so chosen since the site never seemed to
have any of the tender loving care that others in the cemetery got
on a regular basis. The ladies planted a variety of flowers both
along that drive and near those headstones.

While most of the flowers that the ladies planted were annuals,
they also did a number of the headstones with Lilies of the Valley.

One of the headstones adorned with new Lilies of the Valley was
Rose's. At the time of the planting no one either knew or cared
about Rose's preference for roses.

That lack of interest or knowledge about Rose came to an abrupt
halt when those Lilies of the Valley bloomed.

They looked like Lilies of the Valley, they had that same small delicate flower that any other Lilies of the Valley had. What they had, unlike any others, was the distinct red of red roses, and the odor of roses.

Out of the remarkable event of rose colored Lilies of the Valley came investigation of the gravesite and its occupant. This investigation led to the committee learning about Rose and her hobby of roses.

 Somehow, that issue raised some contention within the committee, and the decision was made to dig those delicate little Lilies of the Valley up and replant that particular gravesite with some other flower.

We don't know what that second flower was but the reports was that it was a most unrose type of flower . . . . . but bloomed that luxurious red rose color and smelled like roses.

Imagination and adventure have never been the strong suits of committees, be they little old ladies, or some other kind of committee.

Unfortunately, that committee was apparently pretty much true to type, and chose to solve the whole mystery by striking that particular gravesite from their flower planting program.

The author made a half-hearted stab at doing the research to find the gravesite of a Rose McDonald in a cemetery on Grand Island . . . . but to no avail.

So, we don't know how Rose's ghost pulled that off, or if she still would today if flowers were planted there again.

I guess I am of the opinion that it would be nice if Rose still had her way and could work magic with flowers, turning the anemic and shy little Lily of the Valley into a bright red rose.

## CHAPTER XVII

## OVER THE EDGE

his story in this book about ghosts of the Niagara River is somewhat of a rarity. It is a story of the ghost of an animal.

Most ghost stories involve the ghost of a human, but on occasion, we find a story about an animal, usually a cat, a horse or a dog.

This story is one about a ghost dog. This writer was unable to get very good information about when it happened, or exactly where in the falls area it happened.

The story as I understand is one that involves a family fishing from a rowboat, apparently quite a few years ago.

It seems that the family was out in the boat fishing. Apparently the outing was taking place closer to the falls than is allowed today. The story goes to the effect that the family consisted of the parents and a couple of kids.

The family was doing pretty well in their fishing and were getting quite a few fish that summer afternoon. Rather than to put the fish on a stringer they simply pitched the critters down onto the floor of the boat.

Those fish did what fish do, and occupied their time flopping around and splashing in the little water that was in the boat.

Well, those floppy fish and splashing water was said to be almost more than the ankle biter could handle, and got pretty hyped up over the whole affair.

It was, as I say, one of those high strung little dogs. It must not have taken much to work that pooch into a frenzy of excitement.

The kids didn't help any, they did what they could to get that dog charged up as much as they could just for the fun of seeing the animal get more and more excited about those fish down there thrashing around, doing their flip-floppin', splashing and generally making a mess of that little dog's self-control.

Finally in a frenzy of excitement, the dog simply jumped over the side and swam down-stream to the not too distant falls.

The man's inclination to row down after the mutt met with fierce opposition from his wife, she being afraid they might well join their dog in a long fall down.

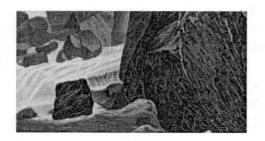

So, The family let the go, and sure enough it was swept over the falls. The whole thing happened close enough to the shore that some folks on shore near the falls could hear the poor animal yip as it plunged downward.

The dog's remains never were found, and the situation there at the falls about the time a little ankle biter was swept over the falls was soon forgotten.

But, a year later, the incident was remembered because on a day much like that fateful day the year earlier, some folks heard coming from the falls, those same yips emitted by that poor animal on the day of its death.

Several times since then, on a lazy summer afternoon, just the kind of afternoon it can be great for fishing, visitors at the falls, and employees have heard the yips and yelps of a little dog coming from the waters as it plunges over the edge.

We hope that the poor animal doesn't have to relive what was undoubtedly a terrifying experience time after time, but that could well be what is going on.

# The Inconvenience

When Ben and Alice bought that old brick house, they neither knew nor cared about the history of the place. All they knew was that the price was right, and it would make one heck of a nice B&B.

It was a fixer-upper without a doubt, and would involve a lot of work to bring it up to a quality appropriate for a B&B. Still, they thought it was the opportunity of a lifetime.

So, this couple bought the old Victorian mansion, and started down the long road of repairing it and restoring its 1800's beauty.

*Ok, I'm lying about this being appropriate for this book. The circumstances detailed in this story didn't happen near here at all. This story really comes to us from London, Kentucky, on I-75.*

*But, I'm putting this story in this book anyway because it's such a good one. What I'm depending on is that the reader won't read this little bitty print in this footnote...or if he does, that he'll forgive my transgression in putting this story in this book.*

*Thanks for your indulgence.*

In order to save money, the couple decided to live in the place while they were doing the refurbishing. During the course of their work, they found out a bit of the history of the place as they would visit with the neighbors.

The fact that it had been a house of ill repute back in the 1800s didn't really make any difference to them. After almost a hundred years of the house having been a private residence, neither Ben nor Alice expected anyone to confuse their new place with a house of ill repute.

The work progressed slowly as it always does when you are trying to bootstrap a project.

And, of course, there were any number of times that problems arose that gave them second thoughts about the wisdom of doing the project.

It was Ben who was most easily discouraged by the setbacks they would encounter.

Alice, on the other hand, was more inclined to take the long view, and to realize that when they got done with it, it would be a beautiful place, well worth the time and money to make it all happen.

During each of those times that Ben would question if they should continue, Alice would counter with her standard answer... "It'll all work out alright."

Ben could just about depend on hearing that...

"It'll all work out alright" whenever he'd suggest they sell the place, and move on.

Then, one night, an event took place that changed everything. It was after a hard day's work that Ben had gone to bed early. He was bushed, and all he wanted to do was hit the sack and get some sleep.

He had just crawled into bed, fluffed his pillow up to his liking and closed his eyes.

Suddenly, as he laid there on his side ready to go to sleep, he felt someone get into bed with him. This sort of surprised Ben because Alice had, just a few minutes earlier, told him that she was going to stay up and put one more coat of varnish on some woodwork they were working on.

Besides that, Alice had a habit of getting into bed as if she were mad at it. Ben had often told her that she got into bed like a 70 pound keg of nails.

His bedmate there sure didn't get into bed that way. It was a matter of kind of gently sliding into bed.

As Ben laid there, about to question Alice why she decided to come to bed after all, the second surprise came along. That surprise was in the form of a warm and gentle puff of breath on the back of his neck.

Now, Ben had been married long enough to know that Alice gently easing into bed, and giving him a provocative puff on his neck was totally out of character for her.

He turned to face her, and found a..........nothing, nothing at all. He had the bed all to himself, no wife, and no warm breath on the back of his neck.

Ben marveled at how he could be dreaming such a thing, not two minutes after laying down. He decided that he was even more tired than he thought, and had gotten to sleep as soon as he got that pillow squared away.

Ben went on to sleep with no further ado.

And, the project of fixing that house up continued. Ben was convinced that it was a never-ending job, and they'd be staining woodwork and hanging wallpaper when they were old and grey. But, he never did come up with a rebuttal to "It'll all work out alright."

It was about two weeks later, and Ben went to bed early again. He wasn't dead tired this time like the last time he had crawled in the sack alone, but just thought he'd get to bed early, and get up early.

The same routine...the laying on his side and the punching around on the pillow until it felt just right.

This time Ben hadn't yet even closed his eyes, and again there was that gentle sliding into bed next to him, followed by a provocative warm breath on the back of his neck.

Wow, this was just like that dream he had a couple weeks earlier, except this time he was awake. Ben wondered why Alice had suddenly taken up behavior that was so out of character for her.

"What's with your sliding into bed that way, Honey? What happened to your hitting the sack like you're mad at it?"

No answer.

"Honey, what's with your sneaking into bed that way?"

Again, no answer.

Twice he had talked to her, and she hadn't answered either time, so he turned so he could see her.............No Alice.........no anybody.

This time Ben knew he had something on his hands other than simply dreaming. Something was going on that needed explanation.

Ben laid there a moment, studying the pillow next to him when the thought struck him that this might be the work of a ghost. Alice was alive and well, he could hear her rattling the

dishes out in the kitchen as she cleaned up after their supper. It couldn't be Alice's ghost 'cause she wouldn't have one.

It was at that moment that he put two and two together and came up with the theory that his bedmate, temporary as she was, was the ghost of one of those fallen doves who had inhabited the house almost a hundred years earlier.

Now, good lookin' honeys softly sliding into bed with a fellow and puffing warm breath on his neck is something of a cause for celebration, even if she is a ghost.

Ben contemplated the situation as he laid there, about as wide awake as one person could be. He came to the conclusion that this house was a good idea, even if it was a lot of work and expense.

Sometimes there are intangible rewards in taking on a project, don't you know.

So, it was off to sleep for Ben, thinking of this good looking raven-haired beauty that had crawled into bed with him. Okay, so he made up the raven-haired part, but sometimes you have to improvise, you know.

Ben developed a new concern. He was concerned about the possibility that his experience that resulted from him going to bed early was not going to be repeated. He need not have feared that. From that point on, that happened a number of times.

Ben didn't bother Alice with all that. She had a lot on her mind, and he didn't want to unduly concern her. Ben was very considerate that way.

But, he chose to tell his buddies about his ghostly visitor. Actually, it was more of a case of bragging to his buddies about that.

Alice noticed that her husband had fewer bouts of wishing they hadn't gotten started on the B&B project. She was glad he was finally coming to see that things will all work out alright.

You know how things are. A buddy will tell his wife things, then his wife will talk to Alice and next thing you know, Alice knows all about the warm-breathed Honey.

It took some tall talking on Ben's part of explaining all that. He put it in the context of a dream, and how he only dreamed all that stuff, and he was really getting tired of having that same old tired dream every once in a while.

Ben took the precaution of holding his hand behind his back and crossing his fingers. He recalled that was a sure fire way of making it perfectly OK to cancel out the moral problem of telling a lie. He remembered that from his childhood. Everybody knew it was OK to lie if you crossed your fingers while doing so.

Surprisingly enough, Alice bought that. Perhaps she had been sniffing too many varnish fumes and didn't realize that Ben was lying through his teeth. They weren't dreams at all, much less dreams that Ben had tired of.

So, Alice put all that behind her. Besides that, you can't blame a fellow for having bad dreams, even if they are dreams about a ghost of a red-headed Honey. Ben had no idea where the "red headed" part came from, but figured that one of his buddies got the story wrong.

In spite of Alice's steadfast nature, the problems of redoing a large old Victorian house started to wear thin for her. So, when they discovered a leak in the roof that would require some expensive repair work, she wondered if they ought to give it up.

"You know, Ben, maybe what we ought to do is sell this place. You've been saying that for a long time now, and I think that maybe you're right."

Oops, this was a development that Ben wasn't ready for, much less come up with an argument against. He knew it was going to take some fancy footwork on his part to jump over to the other side of this "leave" or "not leave" issue.

"Yeah, well, we need to think about that, of course."

It was the best response Ben could come up with since he didn't have time there at the kitchen table to do the fancy footwork he needed to in order to switch sides on that issue.

"After all, Ben, when folks are paying a good price to stay in our B&B, they sure aren't going to appreciate what feels like a little honey crawling in bed with them and puffing warm breath on the back of their necks."

"Oh, no, of course not," Ben replied, hoping that he sounded half way sincere.

Having what seemed like Ben's agreement, Alice went on about how guys sure wouldn't want that inconvenience after a day's driving behind them, and another day's driving ahead of them.

Ben couldn't help but to think to himself..."What an inconvenience! What an inconvenience!"

This story took an unexpected turn as Ben was telling it to me.

"So, did Alice ever catch on to you?"

I had learned earlier from Ben that Alice had passed away shortly after the two of them finished up their B&B project. So, I wondered if she had learned about their ghost before she died.

"No," Ben said, "She never learned the truth, but there is sort of a sequel to this whole story."

"What's that?" I asked.

"Well, it wasn't long after Alice left us that those visits took on a new twist. The new twist was that if I'd go to be early, on occasion, I'd feel someone get into bed beside me, but after I lost Alice, it wasn't a matter of sliding into bed. It was still a ghost 'cause she'd be gone when I turned over."

"How, then, was it different?" I asked.

"It was different because after I lost Alice, my bed partner would get into bed like a 70 pound keg of nails........just like she was mad at the bed."

# My Own Ghost Hunting Notes

# My Own Ghost Hunting Notes

# My Own Ghost Hunting Notes

# My Own Ghost Hunting Notes

# My Own Ghost Hunting Notes

# My Own Ghost Hunting Notes

# My Own Ghost Hunting Notes

# My Own Ghost Hunting Notes

*GHOSTS OF INTERSTATE 90* Chicago to Boston  by D. Latham

*GHOSTS of the Whitewater Valley* by Chuck Grimes

**GHOSTS of Interstate 74**        by B. Carlson

GHOSTS of the Ohio Lakeshore Counties  by Karen Waltemire

*GHOSTS of Interstate 65*        by Joanna Foreman

**GHOSTS of Interstate 25**  by Bruce Carlson

**GHOSTS of the Smoky Mountains** by Larry Hillhouse

GHOSTS of the Illinois Canal System  by David Youngquist

*GHOSTS of the Niagara River*  by Bruce Carlson

**Ghosts of Little Bavaria**        by Kishe Wallace

Shown above (at 85% of actual size) are the spines of other Quixote Press books of ghost stories.
These are available at the retailer from whom this book was procured, or from our office at 1-800-571-2665 cost is $9.95 +
$3.50 S/H.

| | |
|---|---|
| Ghosts of Interstate 75 | by Bruce Carlson |
| *Ghosts of Lake Michigan* | by Ophelia Julien |
| **Ghosts of I-10** | by C. J. Mouser |
| *GHOSTS OF INTERSTATE 55* | by Bruce Carlson |
| Ghosts of US - 13, Wisconsin Dells to Superior | David youngquist   by Bruce Carlson |
| **Ghosts of I-80** | |
| *Ghosts of Interstate 95* | by Bruce Carlson |
| Ghosts of US 550 | by Richard DeVore |
| *Ghosts of Erie Canal*   by Tony Gerst | |
| Ghosts of the Ohio River  by Bruce Carlson | |
| **Ghosts of Warren County**   by Various Writers | |
| Ghosts of I-71 Louisville, KY to Cleveland,OH   by Bruce Carlson | |

**GHOSTS of Lookout Mountain** by Larry Hillhouse

*GHOSTS of Interstate 77* by Bruce Carlson

**GHOSTS of Interstate 94** by B. Carlson

**GHOSTS of MICHIGAN'S U. P.** by Chris Shanley-Dillman

GHOSTS of the FOX RIVER VALLEY by D. Latham

*GHOSTS ALONG I-35* by B. Carlson

**Ghostly Tales of Lake Huron** by Roger H. Meyer

Ghost Stories by Kids, for Kids by some really great fifth graders

Ghosts of Door County Wisconsin by Geri Rider

*Ghosts of the Ozarks* *B Carlson*

**Ghosts of US - 63** by Bruce Carlson

*Ghostly Tales of Lake Erie* by Jo Lela Pope Kimber

*GHOSTS OF DALLAS COUNTY*    by Lori Pielak

**Ghosts of US - 66 from Chicgo to Oklahoma**    By McCarty & Wilson

Ghosts of the Appalachian Trail    by Dr. Tirstan Perry

**Ghosts of I-70**    by B. Carlson

Ghosts of the Thousand Islands    by Larry Hillhouse

*Ghosts of US - 23 in Michigan*    by B. Carlson

**Ghosts of Lake Superior**    by Enid Cleaves

*GHOSTS OF THE IOWA GREAT LAKES*    by Bruce Carlson

*Ghosts of the Amana Colonies*    by Lori Erickson

**Ghosts of Lee County, Iowa**    by Bruce Carlson

The Best of the Mississippi River Ghosts    by Bruce Carlson

**Ghosts of Polk County Iowa**    by Tom Welch

Ghosts of Ohio's Lake Erie shores & Islands Vacationland  by B. Carlson

Ghosts of Des Moines County      by Bruce Carlson

Ghosts of the Wabash River    by Bruce Carlson

Ghosts of Michigan's US 127      by Bruce Carlson

*GHOSTS OF I-79*          *BY BRUCE CARLSON*

*Ghosts of US-66 from Ft. Smith to Flagstaff*    by Connie Wilson

**Ghosts of US 6 in Pennslyvania    by Bruce Carlson**

Ghosts of the Lower Missouri        by Marcia Schwartz

Ghosts of the Tennessee River in Tennessee    by Bruce Carlson

**Ghosts of the Tennessee River in Alabama**

**Ghosts of Michigan's US 12** by R. Rademacher & B. Carlson

Ghosts of the Upper Savannah River from Augusta to Lake Hartwell   by Bruce Carlson

**Mysteries of the Lake of the Ozarks**    Hean & Sugar Hardin

## To Order Copies

Please send me _____copies of *Ghosts of the Niagara River* at $9.95 each plus $3.00 for the first book and $.50 for each additional copy for S/H. (Make checks payable to QUIXOTE **PRESS**.)

Name _____

Street _____

City _____ State _____ Zip _____

**QUIXOTE PRESS**
**3544 Blakslee Street**
**Wever IA 52658**
**1-800-571-2665**

------------------------------------------------

## To Order Copies

Please send me _____copies of *Ghosts of the Niagara River* at $9.95 each plus $3.00 for the first book and $.50 for each additional copy for S/H. (Make checks payable to QUIXOTE **PRESS**.)

Name _____

Street _____

City _____ State _____ Zip _____

QUIXOTE PRESS
**3544 Blakslee Street**
**Wever IA 52658**
**1-800-571-2665**